The Stars, My Brothers

The Stars, My Brothers

by Edmond Hamilton

1.

Something tiny went wrong, but no one ever knew whether it was in an electric relay or in the brain of the pilot.

The pilot was Lieutenant Charles Wandek, UNRC, home address: 1677 Anstey Avenue, Detroit. He did not survive the crash of his ferry into Wheel Five. Neither did his three passengers, a young French astrophysicist, an East Indian expert on magnetic fields, and a forty-year-old man from Philadelphia who was coming out to replace a pump technician.

Someone else who did not survive was Reed Kieran, the only man in Wheel Five itself to lose his life. Kieran, who was thirty-six years old, was an accredited scientist-employee of UNRC. Home address: 815 Elm Street, Midland Springs, Ohio.

Kieran, despite the fact that he was a confirmed bachelor, was in Wheel Five because of a woman. But the woman who had sent him there was no beautiful lost love. Her name was Gertrude Lemmiken; she was nineteen years old and overweight, with a fat, stupid face. She suffered from head-colds, and sniffed constantly in the Ohio college classroom where Kieran taught Physics Two.

One March morning, Kieran could bear it no longer. He told himself, "If she sniffs this morning, I'm through. I'll resign and join the UNRC."

Gertrude sniffed. Six months later, having finished his training for the United Nations Reconnaissance Corps, Kieran shipped out for a term of duty in UNRC Space Laboratory Number 5, known more familiarly as Wheel Five.

Wheel Five circled the Moon. There was an elaborate base on the surface of the Moon in this year 1981. There were laboratories and observatories there, too. But it had been found that the alternating fortnights of boiling heat and near-absolute-zero cold on the lunar surface could play havoc with the delicate instruments used in certain researches. Hence Wheel Five had been built and was staffed by research men who were rotated at regular eight-month intervals.

Kieran loved it, from the first. He thought that that was because of the sheer beauty of it, the gaunt, silver deaths-head of the Moon forever turning beneath, the still and solemn glory of the undimmed stars, the filamentaries stretched across the distant star-clusters like shining veils, the quietness, the peace.

But Kieran had a certain intellectual honesty, and after a while he admitted to himself that neither the beauty nor the romance of it was what made this life so attractive to him. It was the fact that he was far away from Earth. He did not even have to look at Earth, for nearly all geophysical research was taken care of by Wheels Two and

Three that circled the mother planet. He was almost completely divorced from all Earth's problems and people.

Kieran liked people, but had never felt that he understood them. What seemed important to them, all the drives of ordinary day-to-day existence, had never seemed very important to him. He had felt that there must be something wrong with him, something lacking, for it seemed to him that people everywhere committed the most outlandish follies, believed in the most incredible things, were swayed by pure herd-instinct into the most harmful courses of behavior. They could not all be wrong, he thought, so he must be wrong—and it had worried him. He had taken partial refuge in pure science, but the study and then the teaching of astrophysics had not been the refuge that Wheel Five was. He would be sorry to leave the Wheel when his time was up.

And he was sorry, when the day came. The others of the staff were already out in the docking lock in the rim, waiting to greet the replacements from the ferry. Kieran, hating to leave, lagged behind. Then, realizing it would be churlish not to meet this young Frenchman who was replacing him, he hurried along the corridor in the big spoke when he saw the ferry coming in.

He was two-thirds of the way along the spoke to the rim when it happened. There was a tremendous crash that flung him violently from his feet. He felt a coldness, instant and terrible.

He was dying.

He was dead.

The ferry had been coming in on a perfectly normal approach when the tiny something went wrong, in the ship or in the judgment of the pilot. Its drive-rockets suddenly blasted on full, it heeled over sharply, it smashed through the big starboard spoke like a knife through butter.

Wheel Five staggered, rocked, and floundered. The automatic safety bulkheads had all closed, and the big spoke—Section T2—was the only section to blow its air, and Kieran was the only man caught in it. The alarms went off, and while the wreckage of the ferry, with three dead men in it, was still drifting close by, everyone in the Wheel was in his pressure-suit and emergency measures were in full force.

Within thirty minutes it became evident that the Wheel was going to survive this accident. It was edging slowly out of orbit from the impetus of the blow, and in the present weakened state of the construction its small corrective rockets could not be used to stop the drift. But Meloni, the UNRC captain commanding, had got first reports from his damage-control teams, and it did not look too bad. He fired off peremptory demands for the repair materials he would need, and was assured by

UNRC headquarters at Mexico City that the ferries would be loaded and on their way as soon as possible.

Meloni was just beginning to relax a little when a young officer brought up a minor but vexing problem. Lieutenant Vinson had headed the small party sent out to recover the bodies of the four dead men. In their pressure-suits they had been pawing through the tangled wreckage for some time, and young Vinson was tired when he made his report.

"We have all four alongside, sir. The three men in the ferry were pretty badly mangled in the crash. Kieran wasn't physically wounded, but died from space-asphyxiation."

The captain stared at him. "Alongside? Why didn't you bring them in? They'll go back in one of the ferries to Earth for burial."

"But—" Vinson started to protest.

Meloni interrupted sharply. "You need to learn a few things about morale, Lieutenant. You think it's going to do morale here any good to have four dead men floating alongside where everyone can see them? Fetch them in and store them in one of the holds."

Vinson, sweating and unhappy now, had visions of a black mark on his record, and determined to make his point.

"But about Kieran, sir—he was only frozen. Suppose there was a chance to bring him back?"

"Bring him back? What the devil are you talking about?"

Vinson said, "I read they're trying to find some way of restoring a man that gets space-frozen. Some scientists down at Delhi University. If they succeeded, and if we had Kieran still intact in space—"

"Oh, hell, that's just a scientific pipe-dream, they'll never find a way to do that," Meloni said. "It's all just theory."

"Yes, sir," said Vinson, hanging his head.

"We've got trouble enough here without you bringing up ideas like this," the captain continued angrily. "Get out of here."

Vinson was now completely crushed. "Yes, sir. I'll bring the bodies in."

He went out. Meloni stared at the door, and began to think. A commanding officer had to be careful, or he could get skinned alive. If, by some remote chance, this Delhi idea ever succeeded, he, Meloni, would be in for it for having Kieran buried. He strode to the door and flung it open, mentally cursing the young snotty who had had to bring this up.

"Vinson!" he shouted.

The lieutenant turned back, startled. "Yes, sir?"

"Hold Kieran's body outside. I'll check on this with Mexico City."

"Yes, sir."

Still angry, Meloni shot a message to Personnel at Mexico City. That done, he forgot about it. The buck had been passed, let the boys sitting on their backsides down on Earth handle it.

Colonel Hausman, second in command of Personnel Division of UNRC, was the man to whom Meloni's message went. He snorted loudly when he read it. And later, when he went in to report to Garces, the brigadier commanding the Division, he took the message with him.

"Meloni must be pretty badly rattled by the crash," he said. "Look at this."

Garces read the message, then looked up. "Anything to this? The Delhi experiments, I mean?"

Hausman had taken care to brief himself on that point and was able to answer emphatically.

"Damned little. Those chaps in Delhi have been playing around freezing insects and thawing them out, and they think the process might be developed someday to where it could revive frozen spacemen. It's an iffy idea. I'll burn Meloni's backside off for bringing it up at a time like this."

Garces, after a moment, shook his head. "No, wait. Let me think about this."

He looked speculatively out of the window for a few moments. Then he said,

"Message Meloni that this one chap's body—what's his name, Kieran?—is to be preserved in space against a chance of future revival."

Hausman nearly blotted his copybook by exclaiming, "For God's sake—" He choked that down in time and said, "But it could be centuries before a revival process is perfected, if it ever is."

Garces nodded. "I know. But you're missing a psychological point that could be valuable to UNRC. This Kieran has relatives, doesn't he?"

Hausman nodded. "A widowed mother and a sister. His father's been dead a long time. No wife or children."

Garces said, "If we tell them he's dead, frozen in space and then buried, it's all over with. Won't those people feel a lot better if we tell them that he's apparently dead, but might be brought back when a revival-technique is perfected in the future?"

"I suppose they'd feel better about it," Hausman conceded. "But I don't see—"

Garces shrugged. "Simple. We're only really beginning in space, you know. As we go on, UNRC is going to lose a number of men, space-struck just like Kieran. A howl will go up about our casualty lists, it always does. But if we can say that they're only frozen until such time as revival technique is achieved, everyone will feel better about it."

"I suppose public relations are important—" Hausman began to say, and Garces nodded quickly.

"They are. See that this is done, when you go up to confer with Meloni. Make sure that it gets onto the video networks, I want everyone to see it."

Later, with many cameras and millions of people watching, Kieran's body, in a pressure-suit, was ceremoniously taken to a selected position where it would orbit the Moon. All suggestions of the funerary were carefully avoided. The space-struck man—nobody at all referred to him as "dead"—would remain in this position until a revival process was perfected.

"Until forever," thought Hausman, watching sourly. "I suppose Garces is right. But they'll have a whole graveyard here, as time goes on."

As time went on, they did.

2.

In his dreams, a soft voice whispered.

He did not know what it was telling him, except that it was important. He was hardly aware of its coming, the times it came. There would be the quiet murmuring, and something in him seemed to hear and understand, and then the murmur faded away and there was nothing but the dreams again.

But were they dreams? Nothing had form or meaning. Light, darkness, sound, pain and not-pain, flowed over him. Flowed over—who?

Who was he? He did not even know that. He did not care.

But he came to care, the question vaguely nagged him. He should try to remember. There was more than dreams and the whispering voice. There was—what? If he had one real thing to cling to, to put his feet on and climb back from— One thing like his name.

He had no name. He was no one. Sleep and forget it. Sleep and dream and listen—

"Kieran."

It went across his brain like a shattering bolt of lightning, that word. He did not know what the word was or what it meant but it found an echo somewhere and his brain screamed it.

"Kieran!"

Not his brain alone, his voice was gasping it, harshly and croakingly, his lungs seeming on fire as they expelled the word.

He was shaking. He had a body that could shake, that could feel pain, that was feeling pain now. He tried to move, to break the nightmare, to get back again to the vague dreams, and the soothing whisper.

He moved. His limbs thrashed leadenly, his chest heaved and panted, his eyes opened.

He lay in a narrow bunk in a very small metal room.

He looked slowly around. He did not know this place. The gleaming white metal of walls and ceiling was unfamiliar. There was a slight, persistent tingling vibration in everything that was unfamiliar, too.

He was not in Wheel Five. He had seen every cell in it and none of them were like this. Also, there lacked the persistent susurrant sound of the ventilation pumps. Where—

You're in a ship, Kieran. A starship.

Something back in his mind told him that. But of course it was ridiculous, a quirk of the imagination. There weren't any starships.

You're all right, Kieran. You're in a starship, and you're all right.

The emphatic assurance came from somewhere back in his brain and it was comforting. He didn't feel very good, he felt dopey and sore, but there was no use worrying about it when he knew for sure he was all right—

The hell he was all right! He was in someplace new, someplace strange, and he felt half sick and he was not all right at all. Instead of lying here on his back listening to comforting lies from his imagination, he should get up, find out what was going on, what had happened.

Of a sudden, memory began to clear. What had happened? Something, a crash, a terrible coldness—

Kieran began to shiver. He had been in Section T2, on his way to the lock, and suddenly the floor had risen under him and Wheel Five had seemed to crash into pieces around him. The cold, the pain—

You're in a starship. You're all right.

For God's sake why did his mind keep telling him things like that, things he believed? For if he did not believe them he would be in a panic, not knowing where he was, how he had come here. There was panic in his mind but there was a barrier against it, the barrier of the soothing reassurances that came from he knew not where.

He tried to sit up. It was useless, he was too weak. He lay, breathing heavily. He felt that he should be hysterical with fear but somehow he was not, that barrier in his mind prevented it.

He had decided to try shouting when a door in the side of the little room slid open and a man came in.

He came over and looked down at Kieran. He was a young man, sandy-haired, with a compact, chunky figure and a flat, hard face. His eyes were blue and intense, and they gave Kieran the feeling that this man was a wound-up spring. He looked down and said,

"How do you feel, Kieran?"

Kieran looked up at him. He asked, "Am I in a starship?"

"Yes."

"But there aren't any starships."

"There are. You're in one." The sandy-haired man added, "My name is Vaillant."

It's true, what he says, murmured the something in Kieran's mind.

"Where—how—" Kieran began.

Vaillant interrupted his stammering question. "As to where, we're quite a way from Earth, heading right now in the general direction of Altair. As to how—" He paused, looking keenly down at Kieran. "Don't you know how?"

Of course I know. I was frozen, and now I have been awakened and time has gone by—

Vaillant, looking searchingly down at his face, showed a trace of relief. "You do know, don't you? For a moment I was afraid it hadn't worked."

He sat down on the edge of the bunk.

"How long?" asked Kieran.

Vaillant answered as casually as though it was the most ordinary question in the world. "A bit over a century."

It was wonderful, thought Kieran, how he could take a statement like that without getting excited. It was almost as though he'd known it all the time.

"How—" he began, when there was an interruption.

Something buzzed thinly in the pocket of Vaillant's shirt. He took out a thin three-inch disk of metal and said sharply into it,

"Yes?"

A tiny voice squawked from the disk. It was too far from Kieran for him to understand what it was saying but it had a note of excitement, almost of panic, in it.

Something changed, hardened, in Vaillant's flat face. He said, "I expected it. I'll be right there. You know what to do."

He did something to the disk and spoke into it again. "Paula, take over here."

He stood up. Kieran looked up at him, feeling numb and stupid. "I'd like to know some things."

"Later," said Vaillant. "We've got troubles. Stay where you are."

He went rapidly out of the room. Kieran looked after him, wondering. Troubles—troubles in a starship? And a century had passed—

He suddenly felt an emotion that shook his nerves and tightened his guts. It was beginning to hit him now. He sat up in the bunk and swung his legs out of it and tried to stand but could not, he was too weak. All he could do was to sit there, shaking.

His mind could not take it in. It seemed only minutes ago that he had been walking along the corridor in Wheel Five. It seemed that Wheel Five must exist, that the Earth, the people, the time he knew, must still be somewhere out there. This could be some kind of a joke, or some kind of psychological experiment. That was it—the space-medicine boys were always making way-out experiments to find out how men would bear up in unusual conditions, and this must be one of them—

A woman came into the room. She was a dark woman who might have been thirty years old, and who wore a white shirt and slacks. She would, he thought, have been good-looking if she had not looked so tired and so edgy.

She came over and looked down at him and said to him,

"Don't try to get up yet. You'll feel better very soon."

Her voice was a slightly husky one. It was utterly familiar to Kieran, and yet he had never seen this woman before. Then it came to him.

"You were the one who talked to me," he said, looking up at her. "In the dreams, I mean."

She nodded. "I'm Paula Ray and I'm a psychologist. You had to be psychologically prepared for your awakening."

"Prepared?"

The woman explained patiently. "Hypnopedic technique—establishing facts in the subconscious of a sleeping patient. Otherwise, it would be too terrific a shock for you when you awakened. That was proved when they first tried reviving space-struck men, forty or fifty years ago."

The comfortable conviction that this was all a fake, an experiment of some kind, began to drain out of Kieran. But if it was true—

He asked, with some difficulty, "You say that they found out how to revive space-frozen men, that long ago?"

"Yes."

"Yet it took forty or fifty years to get around to reviving me?"

The woman sighed. "You have a misconception. The process of revival was perfected that long ago. But it has been used only immediately after a wreck or disaster. Men or women in the old space-cemeteries have not been revived."

"Why not?" he asked carefully.

"Unsatisfactory results," she said. "They could not adjust psychologically to changed conditions. They usually became unbalanced. Some suicides and a number of cases of extreme schizophrenia resulted. It was decided that it was no kindness to the older space-struck cases to bring them back."

"But you brought me back?"

"Yes."

"Why?"

"There were good reasons." She said, clearly, evading that question. She went on quickly. "The psychological shock of awakening would have been devastating, if you were not prepared. So, while you were still under sedation, I used the hypnopedic method on you. Your unconscious was aware of the main facts of the situation before you awoke, and that cushioned the shock."

Kieran thought of himself, lying frozen and dead in a graveyard that was space, bodies drifting in orbit, circling slowly around each other as the years passed, in a macabre sarabande— A deep shiver shook him.

"Because all space-struck victims were in pressure-suits, dehydration was not the problem it could have been," Paula was saying. "But it's still a highly delicate process—"

He looked at her and interrupted roughly. "What reasons?" And when she stared blankly, he added, "You said there were good reasons why you picked me for revival. What reasons?"

Her face became tight and alert. "You were the oldest victim, in point of date. That was one of the determining factors—"

"Look," said Kieran. "I'm not a child, nor yet a savage. You can drop the patronizing professional jargon and answer my question."

Her voice became hard and brittle. "You're new to this environment. You wouldn't understand if I told you."

"Try me."

"All right," she answered. "We need you, as a symbol, in a political struggle we're waging against the Sakae."

"The Sakae?"

"I told you that you couldn't understand yet," she answered impatiently, turning away. "You can't expect me to fill you in on a whole world that's new to you, in five minutes."

She started toward the door. "Oh, no," said Kieran. "You're not going yet."

He slid out of the bunk. He felt weak and shaky but resentment energized his flaccid muscles. He took a step toward her.

The lights suddenly went dim, and a bull-throated roar sounded from somewhere, an appalling sound of raw power. The slight tingling that Kieran had felt in the metal fabric around him abruptly became a vibration so deep and powerful that it dizzied him and he had to grab the stanchion of the bunk to keep from falling.

Alarm had flashed into the woman's face. Next moment, from some hidden speaker in the wall, a male voice yelled sharply,

"Overtaken—prepare for extreme evasion—"

"Get back into the bunk," she told Kieran.

"What is it?"

"It may be," she said with a certain faint viciousness, "that you're about to die a second time."

3.

The lights dimmed to semi-darkness, and the deep vibration grew worse. Kieran clutched the woman's arm.

"What's happening?"

"Damn it, let me go!" she said.

The exclamation was so wholly familiar in its human angriness that Kieran almost liked her, for the first time. But he continued to hold onto her, although he did not feel that with his present weakness he could hold her long.

"I've a right to know," he said.

"All right, perhaps you have," said Paula. "We—our group—are operating against authority. We've broken laws, in going to Earth and reviving you. And now authority is catching up to us."

"Another ship? Is there going to be a fight?"

"A fight?" She stared at him, and shock and then faint repulsion showed in her face. "But of course, you come from the old time of wars, you would think that—"

Kieran got the impression that what he had said had made her look at him with the same feelings he would have had when he looked at a decent, worthy savage who happened to be a cannibal.

"I always felt that bringing you back was a mistake," she said, with a sharpness in her voice. "Let me go."

She wrenched away from him and before he could stop her she had got to the door and slid it open. He woke up in time to lurch after her and he got his shoulder into the door-opening before she could slide it shut.

"Oh, very well, since you insist I'm not going to worry about you," she said rapidly, and turned and hurried away.

Kieran wanted to follow her but his knees were buckling under him. He hung to the side of the door-opening. He felt angry, and anger was all that kept him from falling over. He would not faint, he told himself. He was not a child, and would not be treated like one—

He got his head outside the door. There was a long and very narrow corridor out there, blank metal with a few closed doors along it. One door, away down toward the end of the corridor, was just sliding shut.

He started down the corridor, steadying himself with his hand against the smooth wall. Before he had gone more than a few steps, the anger that pushed him began to ebb away. Of a sudden, the mountainous and incredible fact of his being here, in this place, this time, this ship, came down on him like an avalanche from which the hypnopedic pre-conditioning would no longer protect him.

I am touching a starship, I am in a starship, I, Reed Kieran of Midland Springs, Ohio. I ought to be back there, teaching my classes, stopping at Hartnett's Drug Store for a soft drink on the way home, but I am here in a ship fleeing through the stars ...

His head was spinning and he was afraid that he was going to go out again. He found himself at the door and slid it open and fell rather than walked inside. He heard a startled voice.

This was a bigger room. There was a table whose top was translucent and which showed a bewildering mass of fleeting symbols in bright light, ever changing. There was a screen on one wall of the room and that showed nothing, a blank, dark surface.

Vaillant and Paula Ray and a tall, tough-looking man of middle age were around the table and had looked up, surprised.

Vaillant's face flashed irritation. "Paula, you were supposed to keep him in his cabin!"

"I didn't think he was strong enough to follow," she said.

"I'm not," said Kieran, and pitched over.

The tall middle-aged man reached and caught him before he hit the floor, and eased him into a chair.

He heard, as though from a great distance, Vaillant's voice saying irritatedly, "Let Paula take care of him, Webber. Look at this—we're going to cross another rift—"

There were a few minutes then when everything was very jumbled up in Kieran's mind. The woman was talking to him. She was telling him that they had prepared him physically, as well as psychologically, for the shock of revival, and that he would be quite all right but had to take things more slowly.

He heard her voice but paid little attention. He sat in the chair and blankly watched the two men who hung over the table and its flow of brilliant symbols. Vaillant seemed to tighten up more and more as the moments passed, and there was still about him the look of a coiled spring but now the spring seemed to be wound to the breaking-point. Webber, the tall man with the tough face, watched the fleeting symbols and his face was stony.

"Here we go," he muttered, and both he and Vaillant looked up at the blank black screen on the wall.

Kieran looked too. There was nothing. Then, in an instant, the blackness vanished from the screen and it framed a vista of such cosmic, stunning splendor that Kieran could not grasp it.

Stars blazed like high fires across the screen, loops and chains and shining clots of them. This was not too different from the way they had looked from Wheel Five. But what was different was that the starry firmament was partly blotted out by vast rifted ramparts of blackness, ebon cliffs that went up to infinity. Kieran had seen astronomical photographs like this and knew what the blackness was.

Dust. A dust so fine that its percentage of particles in space would be a vacuum, on Earth. But, here where it extended over parsecs of space, it formed a barrier to light. There was a narrow rift here between the titan cliffs of darkness and he—the ship he was in—was fleeing across that rift.

The screen abruptly went black again. Kieran remained sitting and staring at it. That incredible fleeting vision had finally impressed the utter reality of all this upon his mind. They, this ship, were far from Earth—very far, in one of the dust-clouds in which they were trying to lose pursuers. This was real.

"—will have got another fix on us as we crossed, for sure," Vaillant was saying, in a bitter voice. "They'll have the net out for us—the pattern will be shaping now and we can't slip through it."

"We can't," said Webber. "The ship can't. But the flitter can, with luck."

They both looked at Kieran. "He's the important one," Webber said. "If a couple of us could get him through—"

"No," said Paula. "We couldn't. As soon as they caught the ship and found the flitter gone, they'd be after him."

"Not to Sako," said Webber. "They'd never figure that we'd take him to Sako."

"Do I have a word in this?" asked Kieran, between his teeth.

"What?" asked Vaillant.

"This. The hell with you all. I'll go no place with you or for you."

He got a savage satisfaction from saying it, he was tired of sitting there like a booby while they discussed him, but he did not get the reaction from them he had expected. The two men merely continued to look thoughtfully at him. The woman sighed,

"You see? There wasn't time enough to explain it to him. It's natural for him to react with hostility."

"Put him out, and take him along," said Webber.

"No," said Paula sharply. "If he goes out right now he's liable to stay out. I won't answer for it."

"Meanwhile," said Vaillant with an edge to his voice, "the pattern is forming up. Have you any suggestions, Paula?"

She nodded. "This."

She suddenly squeezed something under Kieran's nose, a small thing that she had produced from her pocket without his noticing it, in his angry preoccupation with the two men. He smelled a sweet, refreshing odor and he struck her arm away.

"Oh, no, you're not giving me any more dopes—"

Then he stopped, for suddenly it all seemed wryly

humorous to him. "A bunch of bloody incompetents," he said, and laughed. "This is the one thing I would never have dreamed—that a man could sleep, and wake up in a starship, and find the starship manned by blunderers."

"Euphoric," said Paula, to the two men.

"At that," said Webber sourly, "there may be something in what he says about us."

Vaillant turned on him and said fiercely, "If that's what you think—" Then he controlled himself and said tightly, "Quarrelling's no good. We're in a box but we can maybe still put it over if we get this man to Sako. Webber, you and Paula take him in the flitter."

Kieran rose to his feet. "Fine," he said gaily. "Let us go in the flitter, whatever that is. I am already bored with starships."

He felt good, very good. He felt a little drunk, not enough to impede his mental processes but enough to give him a fine devil-may-care indifference to what happened next. So it was only the spray Paula had given him—it still made his body feel better and removed his shock and worry and made everything seem suddenly rather amusing.

"Let us to Sako in the flitter," he said. "After all, I'm living on velvet, I might as well see the whole show. I'm sure that Sako, wherever it is, will be just as full of human folly as Earth was."

"He's euphoric," Paula said again, but her face was stricken.

"Of all the people in that space-cemetery, we had to pick one who thinks like that," said Vaillant, with a sort of restrained fury.

"You said yourself that the oldest one would be the best," said Webber. "Sako will change him."

Kieran walked down the corridor with Webber and Paula and he laughed as he walked. They had brought him back from nothingness without his consent, violating the privacy of death or near-death, and now something that he had just said had bitterly disappointed them.

"Come along," he said buoyantly to the two. "Let us not lag. Once aboard the flitter and the girl is mine."

"Oh for God's sake shut up," said Webber.

4.

It was ridiculous to be flying the stars with a bad hangover, but Kieran had one. His head ached dully, he had an unpleasant metallic taste in his mouth, and his former ebullience had given way to a dull depression. He looked sourly around.

He sat in a confined little metal coop of a cabin, hardly enough in which to stand erect. Paula Ray, in a chair a few feet away was sleeping, her head on her breast. Webber sat forward, in what appeared to be a pilot-chair with a number of crowded control banks in front of it. He was not doing anything to the controls. He looked as though he might be sleeping, too.

That was all—a tiny metal room, blank metal walls, silence. They were, presumably, flying between the stars at incredible speeds but there was nothing to show it. There were no screens such as the one he had seen in the ship, to show by artful scanning devices what vista of suns and darknesses lay outside.

"A flitter," Webber had informed him, "just doesn't have room for the complicated apparatus that such scanners require. Seeing is a luxury you dispense with in a flitter. We'll see when we get to Sako."

After a moment he had added, "If we get to Sako."

Kieran had merely laughed then, and had promptly gone to sleep. When he had awakened, it had been with the euphoria all gone and with his present hangover.

"At least," he told himself, "I can truthfully say that this one wasn't my fault. That blasted spray—"

He looked resentfully at the sleeping woman in the chair. Then he reached and roughly shook her shoulder.

She opened her eyes and looked at him, first sleepily and then with resentment.

"You had no right to wake me up," she said.

Then, before Kieran could retort, she seemed to realize the monumental irony of what she had just said, and she burst into laughter.

"I'm sorry," she said. "Go ahead and say it. I had no right to wake you up."

"Let's come back to that," said Kieran after a moment. "Why did you?"

Paula looked at him ruefully. "What I need now is a ten-volume history of the last century, and time enough for you to read it. But since we don't have either—" She broke off, then after a pause asked, "Your date was 1981, wasn't it? It and your name were on the tag of your pressure-suit."

"That's right."

"Well, then. Back in 1981, it was expected that men would spread out to the stars, wasn't it?"

Kieran nodded. "As soon as they had a workable high-speed drive. Several drives were being experimented with even then."

"One of them—the Flournoy principle—was finally made workable," she said. She frowned. "I'm trying to give you this briefly and I keep straying into details."

"Just tell me why you woke me up."

"I'm trying to tell you." She asked candidly, "Were you always so damned hateful or did the revivification process do this to you?"

Kieran grinned. "All right. Go ahead."

"Things happened pretty much as people foresaw back in 1981," she said. "The drive was perfected. The ships went out to the nearer stars. They found worlds. They established colonies from the overflowing population of Earth. They found human indigenous races on a few worlds, all of them at a rather low technical level, and they taught them.

"There was a determination from the beginning to make it one universe. No separate nationalistic groups, no chance of wars. The governing council was set up at Altair Two. Every world was represented. There are twenty-nine of them, now. It's expected to go on like that, till there are twenty-nine hundred starworlds represented there, twenty-nine thousand—any number. But—"

Kieran had been listening closely. "But what? What upset this particular utopia?"

"Sako."

"This world we're going to?"

"Yes," she said soberly. "Men found something different about this world when they reached it. It had people—human people—on it, very low in the scale of civilization."

"Well, what was the problem? Couldn't you start teaching them as you had others?"

She shook her head. "It would take a long while. But that wasn't the real problem. It was— You see, there's another race on Sako beside the human ones, and it's a fairly civilized race. The Sakae. The trouble is—the Sakae aren't human."

Kieran stared at her. "So what? If they're intelligent—"

"You talk as though it was the simplest thing in the world," she flashed.

"Isn't it? If your Sakae are intelligent and the humans of Sako aren't, then the Sakae have the rights on that world, don't they?"

She looked at him, not saying anything, and again she had that stricken look of one who has tried and failed. Then from up forward, without turning, Webber spoke.

"What do you think now of Vaillant's fine idea, Paula?"

"It can still work," she said, but there was no conviction in her voice.

"If you don't mind," said Kieran, with an edge to his voice, "I'd still like to know what this Sako business has to do with reviving me."

"The Sakae rule the humans on that world," Paula answered. "There are some of us who don't believe they should. In the Council, we're known as the Humanity Party, because we believe that humans should not be ruled by non-humans."

Again, Kieran was distracted from his immediate question—this time by the phrase "Non-human".

"These Sakae—what are they like?"

"They're not monsters, if that's what you're thinking of," Paula said. "They're bipeds—lizardoid rather than humanoid—and are a fairly intelligent and law-abiding lot."

"If they're all that, and higher in development than the humans, why shouldn't they rule their own world?" demanded Kieran.

Webber uttered a sardonic laugh. Without turning he asked, "Shall I change course and go to Altair?"

"No!" she said. Her eyes flashed at Kieran and she spoke almost breathlessly. "You're very sure about things you just heard about, aren't you? You know what's right and you know what's wrong, even though you've only been in this time, this universe, for a few hours!"

Kieran looked at her closely. He thought he was beginning to get a glimmer of the shape of things now.

"You—all you who woke me up illegally—you belong to this Humanity Party, don't you? You did it for some reason connected with that?"

"Yes," she answered defiantly. "We need a symbol in this political struggle. We thought that one of the oldtime space pioneers, one of the humans who began the conquest of the stars, would be it. We—"

Kieran interrupted. "I think I get it. It was really considerate of you. You drag a man back from what amounts to death, for a party rally. 'Oldtime space hero condemns non-humans'—it would go something like that, wouldn't it?"

"Listen—," she began.

"Listen, hell," he said. He was hot with rage, shaking with it. "I am glad to say that you could not possibly have picked a worse symbol than me. I have no more use for the idea of the innate sacred superiority of one species over another than I had for that of one kind of man over another."

Her face changed. From an angry woman, she suddenly became a professional psychologist, coolly observing reactions.

"It's not the political question you really resent," she said. "You've wakened to a strange world and you're afraid of it, in spite of all the pre-awakening preparation we gave your subconscious. You're afraid, and so you're angry."

Kieran got a grip on himself. He shrugged. "What you say may be true. But it doesn't change the way I feel. I will not help you one damned bit."

Webber got up from his seat and came back toward them, his tall form stooping. He looked at Kieran and then at the woman.

"We have to settle this right now," he said. "We're getting near enough to Sako to go out of drive. Are we going to land or aren't we?"

"Yes," said Paula steadily. "We're landing."

Webber glanced again at Kieran's face. "But if that's the way he feels—"

"Go ahead and land," she said.

5.

It was nothing like landing in a rocket. First there was the business referred to as "going out of drive". Paula made Kieran strap in and she said, "You may find this unpleasant, but just sit tight. It doesn't last long." Kieran sat stiff and glowering, prepared for anything and determined not to show it no matter how he felt. Then Webber did something to the control board and the universe fell apart. Kieran's stomach came up and stuck in his throat. He was falling—up? Down? Sideways? He didn't know, but whichever it was not all the parts of him were falling at the same rate, or perhaps it was not all in the same direction, he didn't know that either, but it was an exceptionally hideous feeling. He opened his mouth to protest, and all of a sudden he was sitting normally in the chair in the normal cabin and screaming at the top of his lungs.

He shut up.

Paula said, "I told you it would be unpleasant."

"So you did," said Kieran. He sat, sweating. His hands and feet were cold.

Now for the first time he became aware of motion. The flitter seemed to hurtle forward at comet-like speed. Kieran knew that this was merely an ironic little joke, because now they were proceeding at something in the range of normal velocity, whereas before their speed had been quite beyond his comprehension. But he could comprehend this. He could feel it. They were going like a bat out of hell, and somewhere ahead of them was a planet, and he was closed in, blind, a mouse in a nose-cone. His insides writhed with helplessness and the imminence of a crash. He wanted very much to start screaming again, but Paula was watching him.

In a few moments that desire became academic. A whistling shriek began faintly outside the hull and built swiftly to a point where nothing could have been heard above it. Atmosphere. And somewhere under the blind wall of the flitter a rock-hard world-face reeling and rushing, leaping to meet them—

The flitter slowed. It seemed to hang motionless, quivering faintly. Then it dropped. Express elevator in the world's tallest building, top to bottom—only the elevator is a bubble and the wind is tossing it from side to side as it drops and there is no bottom.

They hung again, bounding lightly on the unseen wind.

Then down.

And hang again.

And down.

Paula said suddenly, "Webber. Webber, I think he's dying." She began to unstrap.

Kieran said faintly, "Am I turning green?"

She looked at him, frowning. "Yes."

"A simple old malady. I'm seasick. Tell Webber to quit playing humming-bird and put this thing down."

Paula made an impatient gesture and tightened her belt again.

Hang and drop. Once more, twice more. A little rocking bounce, a light thump, motion ceased. Webber turned a series of switches. Silence.

Kieran said, "Air?"

Webber opened a hatch in the side of the cabin. Light poured in. It had to be sunlight, Kieran knew, but it was a queer color, a sort of tawny orange that carried a pleasantly burning heat. He got loose with Paula helping him and tottered to the hatch. The air smelled of clean sun-warmed dust and some kind of vegetation. Kieran climbed out of the flitter, practically throwing himself out in his haste. He wanted solid ground under him, he didn't care whose or where.

And as his boots thumped onto the red-ochre sand, it occurred to him that it had been a very long time since he had had solid ground underfoot. A very long time indeed—

His insides knotted up again, and this time it was not seasickness but fear, and he was cold all through again in spite of the hot new sun.

He was afraid, not of the present, nor of the future, but of the past. He was afraid of the thing tagged Reed Kieran, the stiff blind voiceless thing wheeling its slow orbit around the Moon, companion to dead worlds and dead space, brother to the cold and the dark.

He began to tremble.

Paula shook him. She was talking but he couldn't hear her. He could only hear the rush of eternal darkness past his ears, the thin squeak of his shadow brushing across the stars. Webber's face was somewhere above him, looking angry and disgusted. He was talking to Paula, shaking his head. They were far away. Kieran was losing them, drifting away from them on the black tide. Then suddenly there was something like an explosion, a crimson flare across the black, a burst of heat against the cold. Shocked and wild, the physical part of him clawed back to reality.

Something hurt him, something threatened him. He put his hand to his cheek and it came away red.

Paula and Webber were yanking at him, trying to get him to move.

A stone whizzed past his head. It struck the side of the flitter with a sharp clack, and fell. Kieran's nervous relays finally connected. He jumped for the open hatch. Automatically he pushed Paula ahead of him, trying to shield her, and she gave him an odd startled look. Webber was already inside. More stones rattled around and one grazed Kieran's thigh. It hurt. His cheek was bleeding freely. He rolled inside the flitter and turned to look back out the hatch. He was mad.

"Who's doing it?" he demanded.

Paula pointed. At first Kieran was distracted by the strangeness of the landscape. The flitter crouched in a vastness of red-ochre sand laced with some low-growing plant that shone like metallic gold in the sunlight. The sand receded in tilted planes lifting gradually to a range of mountains on the right, and dropping gradually to infinity on the left. Directly in front of the flitter and quite literally a stone's throw away was the beginning of a thick belt of trees that grew beside a river, apparently quite a wide one though he could not see much but a tawny sparkling of water. The course of the river could be traced clear back to the mountains by the winding line of woods that followed its bed. The trees themselves were not like any Kieran had seen before. There seemed to be several varieties, all grotesque in shape and exotic in color. There were even some green ones, with long sharp leaves that looked like spearheads.

Exotic or not, they made perfectly adequate cover. Stones came whistling out of the woods, but

Kieran could not see anything where Paula was pointing but an occasional shaking of foliage.

"Sakae?" he asked.

Webber snorted. "You'll know it when the Sakae find us. They don't throw stones."

"These are the humans," Paula said. There was an indulgent softness in her voice that irritated Kieran.

"I thought they were our dear little friends," he said.

"You frightened them."

"I frightened them?"

"They've seen the flitter before. But they're extremely alert to modes of behavior, and they knew you weren't acting right. They thought you were sick."

"So they tried to kill me. Nice fellows."

"Self-preservation," Webber said. "They can't afford the luxury of too much kindness."

"They're very kind among themselves," Paula said defensively. To Kieran she added, "I doubt if they were trying to kill you. They just wanted to drive you away."

"Oh, well," said Kieran, "in that case I wouldn't dream of disappointing them. Let's go."

Paula glared at him and turned to Webber. "Talk to them."

"I hope there's time," Webber grunted, glancing at the sky. "We're sitting ducks here. Keep your patient quiet—any more of that moaning and flopping and we're sunk."

He picked up a large plastic container and moved closer to the door.

Paula looked at Kieran's cheek. "Let me fix that."

"Don't bother," he said. At this moment he hoped the Sakae, whoever and whatever they were, would come along and clap these two into some suitable place for the rest of their lives.

Webber began to "talk".

Kieran stared at him, fascinated. He had expected words—primitive words, perhaps resembling the click-speech of Earth's stone-age survivals, but words of some sort. Webber hooted. It was a soft reassuring sound, repeated over and over, but it was not a word. The rattle of stones diminished, then stopped. Webber continued to make his hooting call. Presently it was answered. Webber turned and nodded at Paula, smiling. He reached into the plastic container and drew forth a handful of brownish objects that smelled to Kieran like dried fruit. Webber tossed these out onto the sand. Now he made a different sound, a grunting and whuffling. There was a silence. Webber made the sound again.

On the third try the people came out of the woods.

In all there were perhaps twenty-five of them. They came slowly and furtively, moving a step or two at a time, then halting and peering, prepared to run. The able-bodied men came first, with one in the lead, a fine-looking chap in early middle age who was apparently the chief. The women, the old men, and the children followed, trickling gradually out of the shadow of the trees but remaining where they could disappear in a flash if alarmed. They were all perfectly naked, tall and slender and large-eyed, their muscles strung for speed and agility rather than massive strength. Their bodies gleamed a light bronze color in the sun, and Kieran noticed that the men were beardless and smooth-skinned. Both men and women had long hair, ranging in color from black to tawny, and very clean and glistening. They were a beautiful people, as deer are a beautiful people, graceful, innocent, and wild. The men came to the dried fruits which had been scattered for them. They picked them up and sniffed them, bit them, then began to eat, repeating the grunt-and-whuffle call. The women and children and old men decided everything was safe and joined them. Webber tossed out more fruit, and then got out himself, carrying the plastic box.

"What does he do next?" whispered Kieran to Paula. "Scratch their ears? I used to tame squirrels this way when I was a kid."

"Shut up," she warned him. Webber beckoned and she nudged him to move out of the flitter. "Slow and careful."

Kieran slid out of the flitter. Big glistening eyes swung to watch him. The eating stopped. Some of the little ones scuttled for the trees. Kieran froze. Webber hooted and whuffled some more and the tension relaxed. Kieran approached the group with Paula. There was suddenly no truth in what he was doing. He was an actor in a bad scene, mingling with impossible characters in an improbable setting. Webber making ridiculous noises and tossing his dried fruit around like a caricature of somebody sowing, Paula with her brisk professionalism all dissolved in misty-eyed fondness, himself an alien in this time and place, and these perfectly normal-appearing people behaving like orang-utans with their fur shaved off. He started to laugh and then thought better of it. Once started, he might not be able to stop.

"Let them get used to you," said Webber softly.

Paula obviously had been here before. She had begun to make noises too, a modified hooting more like a pigeon's call. Kieran just stood still. The people moved in around them, sniffing, touching. There was no conversation, no laughing or giggling even among the little girls. A particularly beautiful young woman stood just behind the chief, watching the strangers with big yellow cat-eyes. Kieran took her to be the man's daughter. He smiled at her. She continued to stare, deadpan and blank-eyed, with no answering flicker of a smile. It was as though she had never seen one before. Kieran shivered. All this silence and unresponsiveness became eerie.

"I'm happy to tell you," he murmured to Paula, "that I don't think much of your little pets?"

She could not allow herself to be sharply angry. She only said, in a whisper, "They are not pets, they are not animals. They—"

She broke off. Something had come over the naked people. Every head had lifted, every eye had turned away from the strangers. They were listening. Even the littlest ones were still.

Kieran could not hear anything except the wind in the trees.

"What—?" he started to ask.

Webber made an imperative gesture for silence. The tableau held for a brief second longer. Then the brown-haired man who seemed to be the leader made a short harsh noise. The people turned and vanished into the trees.

"The Sakae," Webber said. "Get out of sight." He ran toward the flitter. Paula grabbed Kieran's sleeve and pushed him toward the trees.

"What's going on?" he demanded as he ran.

"Their ears are better than ours. There's a patrol ship coming, I think."

The shadows took them in, orange-and-gold-splashed shadows under strange trees. Kieran looked back. Webber had been inside the flitter. Now he tumbled out of the hatch and ran toward them. Behind him the hatch closed and the flitter stirred and then took off all by itself, humming.

"They'll follow it for a while," Webber panted. "It may give us a chance to get away." He and Paula started after the running people.

Kieran balked. "I don't know why I'm running away from anybody."

Webber pulled out a snub-nosed instrument that looked enough like a gun to be very convincing. He pointed it at Kieran's middle.

"Reason one," he said. "If the Sakae catch Paula and me here we're in very big trouble. Reason two—this is a closed area, and you're with us, so you will be in very big trouble." He looked coldly at Kieran. "The first reason is the one that interests me most."

Kieran shrugged. "Well, now I know." He ran.

Only then did he hear the low heavy thrumming in the sky.

6.

The sound came rumbling very swiftly toward them. It was a completely different sound from the humming of the flitter, and it seemed to Kieran to hold a note of menace. He stopped in a small clearing where he might see up through the trees. He wanted a look at this ship or flier or whatever it was that had been built and was flown by non-humans.

But Webber shoved him roughly on into a clump of squat trees that were the color of sherry wine, with flat thick leaves.

"Don't move," he said.

Paula was hugging a tree beside him. She nodded to him to do as Webber said.

"They have very powerful scanners." She pointed with her chin. "Look. They've learned."

The harsh warning barks of the men sounded faintly, then were hushed. Nothing moved, except by the natural motion of the wind. The people crouched among the trees, so still that Kieran would not have seen them if he had not known they were there.

The patrol craft roared past, cranking up speed as it went. Webber grinned. "They'll be a couple of hours at least, overhauling and examining the flitter. By that time it'll be dark, and by morning we'll be in the mountains."

The people were already moving. They headed upstream, going at a steady, shuffling trot. Three of the women, Kieran noticed, had babies in their arms. The older children ran beside their mothers.

Two of the men and several of the women were white-haired. They ran also.

"Do you like to see them run?" asked Paula, with a sharp note of passion in her voice. "Does it look good to you?"

"No," said Kieran, frowning. He looked in the direction in which the sound of the patrol craft was vanishing.

"Move along," Webber said. "They'll leave us far enough behind as it is."

Kieran followed the naked people through the woods, beside the tawny river. Paula and Webber jogged beside him. The shadows were long now, reaching out across the water.

Paula kept glancing at him anxiously, as though to detect any sign of weakness on his part. "You're doing fine," she said. "You should. Your body was brought back to normal strength and tone, before you ever were awakened."

"They'll slow down when it's dark, anyway," said Webber.

The old people and the little children ran strongly.

"Is their village there?" Kieran asked, indicating the distant mountains.

"They don't live in villages," Paula said. "But the mountains are safer. More places to hide."

"You said this was a closed area. What is it, a hunting preserve?"

"The Sakae don't hunt them any more."

"But they used to?"

"Well," Webber said, "a long time ago. Not for food, the Sakae are vegetarians, but—"

"But," said Paula, "they were the dominant race, and the people were simply beasts of the field. When they competed for land and food the people were hunted down or driven out." She swung an expressive hand toward the landscape beyond the trees. "Why do you think they live in this desert, scraping a miserable existence along the watercourses? It's land the Sakae didn't want. Now, of course, they have no objection to setting it aside as a sort of game preserve. The humans are protected, the Sakae tell us. They're living their natural life in their natural environment, and when we demand that a program be—"

She was out of breath and had to stop, panting. Webber finished for her.

"We want them taught, lifted out of this naked savagery. The Sakae say it's impossible."

"Is it true?" asked Kieran.

"No," said Paula fiercely. "It's a matter of pride. They want to keep their dominance, so they simply won't admit that the people are anything more than animals, and they won't give them a chance to be anything more."

There was no more talking after that, but even so the three outlanders grew more and more winded and the people gained on them. The sun went down in a blaze of blood-orange light that tinted the trees in even more impossible colors and set the river briefly on fire. Then night came, and just after the darkness shut down the patrol craft returned, beating up along the winding river bed. Kieran froze under the black trees and the hair lifted on his skin. For the first time he felt like a hunted thing. For the first time he felt a personal anger.

The patrol craft drummed away and vanished. "They won't come back until daylight," Webber said.

He handed out little flat packets of concentrated food from his pockets. They munched as they walked. Nobody said anything. The wind, which had dropped at sundown, picked up from a different quarter and began to blow again. It got cold. After a while they caught up with the people, who had stopped to rest and eat. The babies and old people for whom Kieran had felt a worried pity were in much better shape than he. He drank from the river and then sat down. Paula and Webber sat beside him, on the ground. The wind blew hard from the desert, dry and chill. The trees thrashed overhead. Against the pale glimmer of the water Kieran could see naked bodies moving along the river's edge, wading, bending, grubbing in the mud. Apparently they found things, for he could see that they were eating. Somewhere close by other people were stripping fruit or nuts from the trees. A man picked up a stone and pounded something with a cracking noise, then dropped the stone again. They moved easily in the dark, as though they were used to it. Kieran recognized the leader's yellow-eyed daughter, her beautiful slender height outlined against the pale-gleaming water. She stood up to her ankles in the soft mud, holding something tight in her two hands, eating.

The sweat dried on Kieran. He began to shiver.

"You're sure that patrol ship won't come back?" he asked.

"Not until they can see what they're looking for."

"Then I guess it's safe." He began to scramble around, feeling for dried sticks.

"What are you doing?"

"Getting some firewood."

"No." Paula was beside him in an instant, her hand on his arm, "No, you mustn't do that."

"But Webber said—"

"It isn't the patrol ship, Kieran. It's the people. They—"

"They what?"

"I told you they were low on the social scale. This is one of the basic things they have to be taught. Right now they still regard fire as a danger, something to run from."

"I see," Kieran said, and let the kindling fall. "Very well, if I can't have a fire, I'll have you. Your body will warm me." He pulled her into his arms.

She gasped, more in astonishment, he thought, than alarm. "What are you talking about?"

"That's a line from an old movie. From a number of old movies, in fact. Not bad, eh?"

He held her tight. She was definitely female. After a moment he pushed her away.

"That was a mistake. I want to be able to go on disliking you without any qualifying considerations."

She laughed, a curiously flat little sound. "Was everybody crazy in your day?" she asked. And then, "Reed—"

It was the first time she had used his given name. "What?"

"When they threw the stones, and we got back into the flitter, you pushed me ahead of you. You were guarding me. Why?"

He stared at her, or rather at the pale blur of her standing close to him. "Well, it's always been sort of the custom for the men to— But now that I think of it, Webber didn't bother."

"No," said Paula. "Back in your day women were still taking advantage of the dual standard—demanding complete equality with men but clinging to their special status. We've got beyond that."

"Do you like it? Beyond, I mean."

"Yes," she said. "It was good of you to do that, but—"

Webber said, "They're moving again. Come on."

The people walked this time, strung out in a long line between the trees and the water, where the light was a little better and the way more open. The three outlanders tagged behind, clumsy in their boots and clothing. The long hair of the people blew in the wind and their bare feet padded softly, light and swift.

Kieran looked up at the sky. The trees obscured much of it so that all he could see was some scattered stars overhead. But he thought that somewhere a moon was rising.

He asked Paula and she said, "Wait. You'll see."

Night and the river rolled behind them. The moonlight became brighter, but it was not at all like the moonlight Kieran remembered from long ago and far away. That had had a cold tranquility to it, but this light was neither cold nor tranquil. It seemed somehow to shift color, too, which made it even less adequate for seeing than the white moonlight he was used to. Sometimes as it filtered through the trees it seemed, ice-green, and again it was reddish or amber, or blue.

They came to a place where the river made a wide bend and they cut across it, clear of the trees. Paula touched Kieran's arm and pointed. "Look."

Kieran looked, and then he stopped still. The light was not moonlight, and its source was not a moon. It was a globular cluster of stars, hung in the sky like a swarm of fiery bees, a burning and pulsing of many colors, diamond-white and gold, green and crimson, peacock blue and smoky umber. Kieran stared, and beside him Paula murmured, "I've been on a lot of planets, but none of them have anything like this."

The people moved swiftly on, paying no attention at all to the sky.

Reluctantly Kieran followed them into the obscuring woods. He kept looking at the open sky above the river, waiting for the cluster to rise high so he could see it.

It was some time after this, but before the cluster rose clear of the trees, that Kieran got the feeling that something, or someone, was following them.

7.

He had stopped to catch his breath and shake an accumulation of sand out of his boots. He was leaning against a tree with his back to the wind, which meant that he was facing their back-trail, and he thought he saw a shadow move where there was nothing to cast a shadow. He straightened up with the little trip-hammers of alarm beating all over him, but he could see nothing more. He thought he might have been mistaken. Just the same, he ran to catch up with the others.

The people were moving steadily. Kieran knew that their senses were far keener than his, and they were obviously not aware of any danger other than the basic one of the Sakae. He decided that he must have been seeing things.

But an uneasiness persisted. He dropped behind again, this time on purpose, after they had passed a clearing. He stayed hidden behind a tree-trunk and watched. The cluster-light was bright now but very confusing to the eye. He heard a rustling that he did not think was wind, and he thought that something started to cross the clearing and then stopped, as though it had caught his scent.

Then he thought that he heard rustlings at both sides of the clearing, stealthy sounds of stalking that closed in toward him. Only the wind, he told himself, but again he turned to run. This time he met Paula, coming back to look for him.

"Reed, are you all right?" she asked. He caught her arm and pulled her around and made her run. "What is it? What's the matter?"

"I don't know." He hurried with her until he could see Webber ahead, and beyond him the bare backs and blowing hair of the people. "Listen," he said, "are there any predators here?"

"Yes," Paula said, and Webber turned sharply around.

"Have you seen something?"

"I don't know. I thought I did. I'm not sure."

"Where?"

"Behind us."

Webber made the harsh barking danger call, and the people stopped. Webber stood looking back the way they had come. The women caught the children and the men fell back to where Webber stood. They looked and listened, sniffing the air. Kieran listened too, but now he did not hear any rustlings except the high thrashing of the branches. Nothing stirred visibly and the wind would carry away any warning scent.

The men turned away. The people moved on again. Webber shrugged.

"You must have been mistaken, Kieran."

"Maybe. Or maybe they just can't think beyond the elementary. If they don't smell it, it isn't there. If something is after us it's coming up-wind, the way any hunting animal works. A couple of the men ought to circle around and—"

"Come on," said Webber wearily.

They followed the people beside the river. The cluster was high now, a hive of suns reflected in the flowing water, a kaleidoscopic rippling of colors.

Now the women were carrying the smaller children. The ones too large to be carried were lagging behind a little. So were the aged. Not much, yet. Kieran, conscious that he was weaker than the weakest of these, looked ahead at the dim bulk of the mountains and thought that they ought to be able to make it. He was not at all sure that he would.

The river made another bend. The trail lay across the bend, clear of the trees. It was a wide bend, perhaps two miles across the neck. Ahead, where the trail joined the river again, there was a rocky hill. Something about the outlines of the hill seemed wrong to Kieran, but it was too far away to be sure of anything. Overhead the cluster burned gloriously. The people set out across the sand.

Webber looked back. "You see?" he said. "Nothing."

They went on. Kieran was beginning to feel very tired now, all the artificial strength that had been pumped into him before his awakening was running out. Webber and Paula walked with their heads down, striding determinedly but without joy.

"What do you think now?" she asked Kieran. "Is this any way for humans to live?"

The ragged line of women and children moved ahead of them, with the men in the lead. It was not natural, Kieran thought, for children to be able to travel so far, and then he remembered that the young of non-predacious species have to be strong and fleet at an early age.

Suddenly one of the women made a harsh, shrill cry.

Kieran looked where she was looking, off to the left, to the river and the curving line of trees. A large black shadow slipped across the sand. He looked behind him. There were other shadows, coming with long easy bounds out of the trees, fanning out in a shallow crescent. They reminded Kieran of some animal he had once seen in a zoo, a partly catlike, partly doglike beast, a cheetah he thought it had been called, only the cheetah was spotted like a leopard and these creatures were black, with stiff, upstanding ears. They bayed, and the coursing began.

"Nothing," said Kieran bitterly. "I count seven."

Webber said, "My God, I—"

The people ran. They tried to break back to the river and the trees that could be climbed to safety, but the hunters turned them. Then they fled blindly forward, toward the hill. They ran with all their strength, making no sound. Kieran and Webber ran with them, with Paula between them. Webber seemed absolutely appalled.

"Where's that gun you had?" Kieran panted.

"It's not a gun, only a short-range shocker," he said. "It wouldn't stop these things. Look at them!"

They bounded, sporting around them, howling with a sound like laughter. They were as large as leopards and their eyes glowed in the cluster-light. They seemed to be enjoying themselves, as though hunting was the most delightful game in the world.

One of them ran up to within two feet of Kieran and snapped at him with its great jaws, dodging agilely when he raised his arm. They drove the people, faster and faster. At first the men had formed around the women and children. But the formation began to disintegrate as the weaker ones dropped behind, and no attempt was made to keep it. Panic was stronger than instinct now. Kieran looked ahead. "If we can make it to that hill—"

Paula screamed and he stumbled over a child, a girl about five, crawling on her hands and knees. He picked her up. She bit and thrashed and tore at him, her bare little body hard as whalebone and slippery with sweat. He could not hold onto her. She kicked herself free of his hands and rushed wildly out of reach, and one of the black hunters pounced in and bore her away, shrieking thinly like a fledgling bird in the jaws of a cat.

"Oh my God," said Paula, and covered her head with her arms, trying to shut out sight and sound. He caught her and said harshly, "Don't faint, because I can't carry you." The child's mother, whichever of the women it might have been, did not look back.

An old woman who strayed aside was pulled down and dragged off, and then one of the white-haired men. The hill was closer. Kieran saw now what was wrong with it. Part of it was a building. He was too tired and too sick to be interested, except as it offered a refuge. He spoke to Webber, with great difficulty because he was winded. And then he realized that Webber wasn't there.

Webber had stumbled and fallen. He had started to get up, but the hunters were on him. He was on his hands and knees facing them, screaming at them to get away from him. He had, obviously, had little or no experience with raw violence. Kieran ran back to him, with Paula close behind.

"Use your gun!" he yelled. He was afraid of the black hunters, but he was full of rage and the rage outweighed the fear. He yelled at them, cursing them. He hurled sand into their eyes, and one that was creeping up on Webber from the side he kicked. The creature drew off a little, not frightened but surprised. They were not used to this sort of thing from humans. "Your gun!" Kieran roared again, and Webber pulled the snub-nosed thing out of his pocket. He stood up and said unsteadily, "I told you, it's not a gun. It won't kill anything. I don't think—"

"Use it," said Kieran. "And get moving again. Slowly."

They started to move, and then across the sky a great iron voice spoke like thunder. "Lie down," it said, "please. Lie down flat."

Kieran turned his head, startled. From the direction of the building on the hill a vehicle was speeding toward them.

"The Sakae," said Webber with what was almost a sob of relief. "Lie down."

As he did so, Kieran saw a pale flash shoot out from the vehicle and knock over a hunter still hanging on the flanks of the fleeing people. He hugged the sand. Something went whining and whistling over him, there was a thunk and a screech. It was repeated, and then the iron voice spoke again.

"You may get up now. Please remain where you are." The vehicle was much closer. They were bathed in sudden light. The voice said, "Mr. Webber, you are holding a weapon. Please drop it."

"It's only a little shocker," Webber said, plaintively. He dropped it.

The vehicle had wide tracks that threw up clouds of sand. It came clanking to a halt. Kieran, shading his eyes, thought he distinguished two creatures inside, a driver and a passenger.

The passenger emerged, climbing with some difficulty over the steep step of the track, his tail rattling down behind him like a length of thick cable. Once on the ground he became quite agile, moving with a sort of oddly graceful prance on his powerful legs. He approached, his attention centered on Kieran. But he observed the amenities, placing one delicate hand on his breast and making a slight bow.

"Doctor Ray." His muzzle, shaped something like a duck's bill, nevertheless formed Paula's name tolerably well. "And you, I think, are Mr. Kieran."

Kieran said, "Yes." The star-cluster blazed overhead. The dead beasts lay behind him, the people with their flying hair had run on beyond his sight. He had been dead for a hundred years and now he was alive again. Now he was standing on alien soil, facing an alien form of life, communicating with it, and he was so dog-tired and every sensory nerve was so thoroughly flayed that he had nothing left to react with. He simply looked at the Saka as he might have looked at a fence-post, and said, "Yes."

The Saka made his formal little bow again. "I am Bregg." He shook his head. "I'm glad I was able to reach you in time. You people don't seem to have any notion of the amount of trouble you make for us—"

Paula, who had not spoken since the child was carried off, suddenly screamed at Bregg, "Murderer!"

She sprang at him, striking him in blind hysteria.

8.

Bregg sighed. He caught Paula in those fine small hands that seemed to have amazing strength and held her, at arm's length. "Doctor Ray," he said. He shook her. "Doctor Ray." She stopped screaming. "I don't wish to administer a sedative because then you will say that I drugged you. But I will if I must."

Kieran said, "I'll keep her quiet."

He took her from Bregg. She collapsed against him and began to cry. "Murderers," she whispered. "That little girl, those old people—"

Webber said, "You could exterminate those beasts. You don't have to let them hunt the people like that. It's—it's—"

"Unhuman is the word you want," said Bregg. His voice was exceedingly weary. "Please get into the car."

They climbed in. The car churned around and sped back toward the building. Paula shivered, and Kieran held her in his arms. Webber said after a moment or two, "How did you happen to be here, Bregg?"

"When we caught the flitter and found it empty, it was obvious that you were with the people, and it became imperative to find you before you came to harm. I remembered that the trail ran close by this old outpost building, so I had the patrol ship drop us here with an emergency vehicle."

Kieran said, "You knew the people were coming this way?"

"Of course." Bregg sounded surprised. "They migrate every year at the beginning of the dry season. How do you suppose Webber found them so easily?"

Kieran looked at Webber. He asked, "Then they weren't running from the Sakae?"

"Of course they were," Paula said. "You saw them yourself, cowering under the trees when the ship went over."

"The patrol ships frighten them," Bregg said. "Sometimes to the point of stampeding them, which is why we use them only in emergencies. The people do not connect the ships with us."

"That," said Paula flatly, "is a lie."

Bregg sighed. "Enthusiasts always believe what they want to believe. Come and see for yourself."

She straightened up. "What have you done to them?"

"We've caught them in a trap," said Bregg, "and we are presently going to stick needles into them—a procedure necessitated by your presence, Doctor Ray. They're highly susceptible to imported viruses, as you should remember—one of your little parties of do-gooders succeeded in wiping out a whole band of them not too many years ago. So—inoculations and quarantine."

Lights had blazed up in the area near the building. The car sped toward them.

Kieran said slowly, "Why don't you just exterminate the hunters and have done with them?"

"In your day, Mr. Kieran—yes, I've heard all about you—in your day, did you on Earth exterminate the predators so that their natural prey might live more happily?"

Bregg's long muzzle and sloping skull were profiled against the lights.

"No," said Kieran, "we didn't. But in that case, they were all animals."

"Exactly," said Bregg. "No, wait, Doctor Ray. Spare me the lecture. I can give you a much better reason than that, one even you can't quarrel with. It's a matter of ecology. The number of humans destroyed by these predators annually is negligible but they do themselves destroy an enormous number of small creatures with which the humans compete for their food. If we exterminated the hunters the small animals would multiply so rapidly that the humans would starve to death."

The car stopped beside the hill, at the edge of the lighted area. A sort of makeshift corral of wire fencing had been set up, with wide wings to funnel the people into the enclosure, where a gate was shut on them. Two Sakae were mounting guard as the party from the car approached the corral. Inside the fence Kieran could see the people, flopped around in positions of exhaustion. They did not seem to be afraid now. A few of them were drinking from a supply of water provided for them. There was food scattered for them on the ground.

Bregg said something in his own language to one of the guards, who looked surprised and questioned him, then departed, springing strongly on his powerful legs. "Wait," said Bregg.

They waited, and in a moment or two the guard came back leading one of the black hunting beasts on a chain. It was a female, somewhat smaller than the ones Kieran had fought with, and having a slash of white on the throat and chest. She howled and sprang up on Bregg, butting her great head into his shoulder, wriggling with delight. He petted her, talking to her, and she laughed doglike and licked his cheek.

"They domesticate well," he said. "We've had a tame breed for centuries."

He moved a little closer to the corral, holding tight to the animal's chain. Suddenly she became aware of the people. Instantly the good-natured pet turned into a snarling fury. She reared on her hind legs and screamed, and inside the corral the people roused up. They were not frightened now. They spat and chattered, clawing up sand and pebbles and bits of food to throw through the fence. Bregg handed the chain to the guard, who hauled the animal away by main force.

Paula said coldly, "If your point was that the people are not kind to animals, my answer is that you can hardly blame them."

"A year ago," Bregg said, "some of the people got hold of her two young ones. They were torn to pieces before they could be saved, and she saw it. I can't blame her, either."

He went on to the gate and opened it and went inside. The people drew back from him. They spat at him, too, and pelted him with food and pebbles. He spoke to them, sternly, in the tone of one speaking to unruly dogs, and he spoke words, in his own tongue. The people began to shuffle about uneasily. They stopped throwing things. He stood waiting.

The yellow-eyed girl came sidling forward and rubbed herself against his thigh, head, shoulder and flank. He reached down and stroked her, and she whimpered with pleasure and arched her back.

"Oh, for God's sake," said Kieran, "let's get out of here."

Later, they sat wearily on fallen blocks of cement inside a dusty, shadowy room of the old building. Only a hand-lamp dispelled the gloom, and the wind whispered coldly, and Bregg walked to and fro in his curious prance as he talked.

"It will be a little while before the necessary medical team can be picked up and brought here," he said. "We shall have to wait."

"And then?" asked Kieran.

"First to—" Bregg used a word that undoubtedly named a city of the Sakae but that meant nothing to Kieran, "—and then to Altair Two. This, of course, is a council matter."

He stopped and looked with bright, shrewd eyes at Kieran. "You are quite the sensation already, Mr. Kieran. The whole community of starworlds is already aware of the illegal resuscitation of one of the pioneer spacemen, and of course there is great interest." He paused. "You, yourself, have done nothing unlawful. You cannot very well be sent back to sleep, and undoubtedly the council will want to hear you. I am curious as to what you will say."

"About Sako?" said Kieran. "About—them?" He made a gesture toward a window through which the wind brought the sound of stirring, of the gruntings and whufflings of the corralled people.

"Yes. About them."

"I'll tell you how I feel," Kieran said flatly. He saw Paula and Webber lean forward in the shadows. "I'm a human man. The people out there may be savage, low as the beasts, good for nothing the way they are—but they're human. You Sakae may be intelligent, civilized, reasonable, but you're not human. When I see you ordering them around like beasts, I want to kill you. That's how I feel."

Bregg did not change his bearing, but he made a small sound that was almost a sigh.

"Yes," he said. "I feared it would be so. A man of your times—a man from a world where humans were all-dominant—would feel that way." He turned and looked at Paula and Webber. "It appears that your scheme, to this extent, was successful."

"No, I wouldn't say that," said Kieran.

Paula stood up. "But you just told us how you feel—"

"And it's the truth," said Kieran. "But there's something else." He looked thoughtfully at her. "It was a good idea. It was bound to work—a man of my time was bound to feel just this way you wanted him to feel, and would go away from here crying your party slogans and believing them. But you overlooked something—"

He paused, looking out the window into the sky, at the faint vari-colored radiance of the cluster.

"You overlooked the fact that when you awoke me, I would no longer be a man of my own time—or of any time. I was in darkness for a hundred years—with the stars my brothers, and no man touching me. Maybe that chills a man's feelings, maybe something deep in his mind lives and has time to think. I've told you how I feel, yes. But I haven't told you what I think—"

He stopped again, then said, "The people out there in the corral have my form, and my instinctive loyalty is to them. But instinct isn't enough. It would have kept us in the mud of Earth forever, if it could. Reason took us out to the wider universe. Instinct tells me that those out there are my people. Reason tells me that you—" he looked at Bregg, "—who are abhorrent to me, who would make my skin creep if I touched you, you who go by reason—that you are my real people. Instinct made a hell of Earth for millennia—I say we ought to leave it behind us there in the mud and not let it make a hell of the stars. For you'll run into this same problem over and over again as you go out into the wider universe, and the old parochial human loyalties must be altered, to solve it."

He looked at Paula and said, "I'm sorry, but if anyone asks me, that is what I'll say."

"I'm sorry, too," she said, rage and dejection ringing in her voice. "Sorry we woke you. I hope I never see you again."

Kieran shrugged. "After all, you did wake me. You're responsible for me. Here I am, facing a whole new universe, and I'll need you." He went over and patted her shoulder.

"Damn you," she said. But she did not move away from him.